GW00500251

FLOWER FAIRIES
THE
LITTLE YELLOW BOOK

FLOWER FAIRIES
THE
LITTLE YELLOW BOOK

CICELY MARY BARKER

FREDERICK WARNE

FREDERICK WARNE

Penguin Books Ltd, Harmondsworth, Middlesex, England
New York, Australia, Canada, New Zealand

First Published 1994

1 3 5 7 9 10 8 6 4 2

ISBN 0 7232 4216 X

Printed and bound by
Tien Wah Press, Singapore

CONTENTS

The Gorse Fairy

The Herb Twopence Fairy

The Iris Fairy

The Kingcup Fairy

The Yellow Deadnettle Fairy

The Greater Celandine Fairy

The Black Medick Fairies

The Sow Thistle Fairy

The Tansy Fairy

The Horned Poppy Fairy

The Colt's-Foot Fairy

The Celandine Fairy

The Dandelion Fairy

The Daffodil Fairy

The Primrose Fairy

The Cowslip Fairy

The Marigold Fairy

The Laburnum Fairy

The Buttercup Fairy

The Bird's-Foot Trefoil Fairy

The Toadflax Fairy

The Ragwort Fairy

The Winter Jasmine Fairy

The Winter Aconite Fairy

G

Gorse

◆ THE SONG OF ◆
THE GORSE FAIRIES

"When gorse is out of blossom,"
  (Its prickles bare of gold)
"Then kissing's out of fashion,"
  Said country-folk of old.
Now Gorse is in its glory
  In May when skies are blue,
But when its time is over,
  Whatever shall we do?

O dreary would the world be,
  With everyone grown cold—
Forlorn as prickly bushes
  Without their fairy gold!
But this will never happen:
  At every time of year
You'll find one bit of blossom—
  A kiss from someone dear!

• THE SONG OF •
THE HERB TWOPENCE FAIRY

Have you pennies? I have many:
  Each round leaf of mine's a penny,
Two and two along the stem—
  Such a business, counting them!
(While I talk, and while you listen,
Notice how the green leaves glisten,
Also every flower-cup:
  Don't I keep them polished up?)

Have you *one* name? I have many:
  "Wandering Sailor", "Creeping Jenny",
"Money-wort", and of the rest
  "Strings of Sovereigns" is the best,
(That's my yellow flowers, you see.)
  "Meadow Runagates" is me,
And "Herb Twopence". Tell me which
  Show I stray, and show I'm rich?

Hyacinth, Heliotrope, Honeysuckle, and Hollyhock, are
some more flowers beginning with H.

Herb Twopence

I

Iris

◆ THE SONG OF ◆
THE IRIS FAIRY

I am Iris: I'm the daughter
Of the marshland and the water.
Looking down, I see the gleam
Of the clear and peaceful stream;
Water-lilies large and fair
With their leaves are floating there;
All the water-world I see,
And my own face smiles at me!

(This is the wild Iris.)

◆ THE SONG OF ◆
THE KINGCUP FAIRY

Golden King of marsh and swamp,
Reigning in your springtime pomp,
Hear the little elves you've found
Trespassing on royal ground:—

"Please, your Kingship, we were told
Of your shining cups of gold;
So we came here, just to see—
Not to rob your Majesty!"

Golden Kingcup, well I know
You will smile and let them go!
Yet let human folk beware
How they thieve and trespass there:

Kingcup-laden, they may lose
In the swamp their boots and shoes!

K

Kingcup

X Y

Yellow Deadnettle

• THE SONG OF •
THE YELLOW DEADNETTLE FAIRY

You saucy X! You love to vex
Your next-door neighbour Y:
And just because no flower is yours,
You tease him on the sly.
Straight, yellow, tall,—of Nettles all,
The handsomest is his;
He thinks no ill, and wonders still
What all your mischief is.
Yet have a care! Bad imp, beware
His upraised hand and arm:
Though stingless, he comes leaping—see!—
To save his flower from harm.

• THE SONG OF •
THE GREATER CELANDINE FAIRY

You come with the Spring,
   O swallow on high!
You come with the Spring,
   And so do I.

Your nest, I know,
   Is under the eaves;
While far below
   Are my flowers and leaves.

Yet, to and fro
   As you dart and fly,
You swoop so low
   That you brush me by!

I come with the Spring;
   The wall is my home;
I come with the Spring
   When the swallows come.

(The name "Celandine" comes from the Greek word for
"swallow", and this celandine used sometimes to be called
"swallow-wort". It has orange-coloured juice in its stems,
and is no relation to the Lesser Celandine, which is in *Flower
Fairies of the Spring*; but it is a relation to the Horned Poppy,
which you will find further on in this book.)

The Greater Celandine Fairy

The Black Medick Fairies

• THE SONG OF •
THE BLACK MEDICK FAIRIES

"Why are we called 'Black', sister,
 When we've yellow flowers?"
"I will show you why, brother:
 See these seeds of ours?
Very soon each tiny seed
 Will be turning black indeed!"

◆ THE SONG OF ◆
THE SOW THISTLE FAIRY

I have handsome leaves, and my stalk is tall
   And my flowers are prettily yellow;
Yet nobody thinks me nice at all:
    They think me a tiresome fellow—
      An ugly weed
      And a rogue indeed;
For wherever I happen to spy,
    As I look around,
    That they've dug their ground,
I say to my seeds "Go, fly!"

    And because I am found
    On the nice soft ground,
    A trespassing weed am I!

(But I have heard that Sow Thistle is good rabbit-food, so
perhaps it is not so useless as most people think.)

The Sow Thistle Fairy

The Tansy Fairy

◆ THE SONG OF ◆
THE TANSY FAIRY

In busy kitchens, in olden days,
Tansy was used in a score of ways;
Chopped and pounded,
  when cooks would make
Tansy puddings and tansy cake,
Tansy posset, or tansy tea;
Physic or flavouring tansy'd be.
      People who know
      Have told me so!

That is my tale of the past; today,
Still I'm here by the King's Highway,
Where the air from the fields
  is fresh and sweet,
With my fine-cut leaves and my flowers neat.
Were ever such button-like flowers seen—
Yellow, for elfin coats of green?
      Three in a row—
      I stitch them so!

• THE SONG OF •
THE HORNED POPPY FAIRY

These are the things I love and know:
The sound of the waves, the sight of the sea;
The great wide shore when the tide is low;
Where there's salt in the air, it's home to me—
With my petals of gold—the home for me!

The waves come up and cover the sand,
Then turn at the pebbly slope of the beach;
I feel the spray of them, where I stand,
Safe and happy, beyond their reach—
With my marvellous horns—
    beyond their reach!

The Horned Poppy Fairy

The
Colt's foot
Fairy.

The Colt's-Foot Fairy

◆ THE SONG OF ◆
THE COLT'S-FOOT FAIRY

The winds of March are keen and cold;
I fear them not, for I am bold.

I wait not for my leaves to grow;
They follow after: they are slow.

My yellow blooms are brave and bright;
I greet the Spring with all my might.

◆ THE SONG OF ◆
THE CELANDINE FAIRY

Before the hawthorn leaves unfold,
Or buttercups put forth their gold,
By every sunny footpath shine
The stars of Lesser Celandine.

The
Celandine
Fairy.

The Celandine Fairy

The Dandelion Fairy

◆ THE SONG OF ◆
THE DANDELION FAIRY

Here's the Dandelion's rhyme:
  See my leaves with tooth-like edges;
Blow my clocks to tell the time;
  See me flaunting by the hedges,
In the meadow, in the lane,
  Gay and naughty in the garden;
Pull me up—I grow again,
  Asking neither leave nor pardon.
Sillies, what are you about
  With your spades and hoes of iron?
You can never drive me out—
  Me, the dauntless Dandelion!

◆ THE SONG OF ◆
THE DAFFODIL FAIRY

I'm everyone's darling: the blackbird and
    starling
Are shouting about me from blossoming
    boughs;
For I, the Lent Lily, the Daffy-down-dilly,
Have heard through the country the call to
    arouse.
The orchards are ringing with voices
    a-singing
The praise of my petticoat, praise of my
    gown;
The children are playing, and hark! they are
    saying
That Daffy-down-dilly is come up to town!

The Daffodil Fairy

The Primrose
Fairy.

The Primrose Fairy

◆ THE SONG OF ◆
THE PRIMROSE FAIRY

The Primrose opens wide in spring;
   Her scent is sweet and good:
It smells of every happy thing
   In sunny lane and wood.
I have not half the skill to sing
   And praise her as I should.

She's dear to folk throughout the land;
   In her is nothing mean:
She freely spreads on every hand
   Her petals pale and clean.
And though she's neither proud nor grand,
   She is the Country Queen.

◆ THE SONG OF ◆
THE COWSLIP FAIRY

The land is full of happy birds
And flocks of sheep and grazing herds.

I hear the songs of larks that fly
Above me in the breezy sky.

I hear the little lambkins bleat;
My honey-scent is rich and sweet.

Beneath the sun I dance and play
In April and in merry May.

The grass is green as green can be;
The children shout at sight of me.

The Cowslip Fairy

The Marigold Fairy

✦ THE SONG OF ✦
THE MARIGOLD FAIRY

Great Sun above me in the sky,
So golden, glorious, and high,
My petals, see, are golden too;
They shine, but cannot shine like you.

I scatter many seeds around;
And where they fall upon the ground,
More Marigolds will spring, more flowers
To open wide in sunny hours.

It is because I love you so,
I turn to watch you as you go;
Without your light, no joy could be.
Look down, great Sun, and shine on me!

◆ THE SONG OF ◆
THE LABURNUM FAIRY

All Laburnum's
Yellow flowers
Hanging thick
In happy showers,—
Look at them!
The reason's plain
Why folks call them
"Golden Rain"!
"Golden Chains"
They call them too,
Swinging there
Against the blue.

(After the flowers, the Laburnum has pods with what look
like tiny green peas in them; but it is best not to play with
them, and they must never, never be eaten, as they are
poisonous.)

The Laburnum Fairy

The Buttercup Fairy

◆ THE SONG OF ◆
THE BUTTERCUP FAIRY

'Tis I whom children love the best;
　　My wealth is all for them;
For them is set each glossy cup
　　Upon each sturdy stem.

O little playmates whom I love!
　　The sky is summer-blue,
And meadows full of buttercups
　　Are spread abroad for you.

◆ THE SONG OF ◆
THE BIRD'S-FOOT TREFOIL FAIRY

Here I dance in a dress like flames,
And laugh to think of my comical names.
Hoppetty hop, with nimble legs!
Some folks call me *Bacon and Eggs*!
While other people, it's really true,
Tell me I'm *Cuckoo's Stockings* too!
Over the hill I skip and prance;
I'm *Lady's Slipper*, and so I dance,
Not like a lady, grand and proud,
But to the grasshoppers' chirping loud.
My pods are shaped like a dicky's toes:
That is what *Bird's-Foot Trefoil* shows;
This is my name which grown-ups use,
But children may call me what they choose.

The Bird's-Foot Trefoil Fairy

The Toadflax Fairy

◆ THE SONG OF ◆
THE TOADFLAX FAIRY

The children, the children,
    they call me funny names,
They take me for their darling
    and partner in their games;
They pinch my flowers' yellow mouths,
    to open them and close,
Saying, *Snap-Dragon!*
      Toadflax!
        or, *darling Bunny-Nose!*

The Toadflax, the Toadflax,
    with lemon-coloured spikes,
With funny friendly faces
    that everybody likes,
Upon the grassy hillside
    and hedgerow bank it grows,
And it's *Snap-Dragon* !
      Toadflax!
        and *darling Bunny-Nose!*

• THE SONG OF •
THE RAGWORT FAIRY

Now is the prime of Summer past,
  Farewell she soon must say;
But yet my gold you may behold
  By every grassy way.

And what though Autumn comes apace,
  And brings a shorter day?
Still stand I here, your eyes to cheer,
  In gallant gold array.

The Ragwort Fairy

The Winter Jasmine Fairy

◆ THE SONG OF ◆
THE WINTER JASMINE FAIRY

All through the Summer my leaves were green,
But never a flower of mine was seen;
Now Summer is gone, that was so gay,
And my little green leaves are shed away.
   In the grey of the year
  What cheer, what cheer?

The Winter is come, the cold winds blow;
I shall feel the frost and the drifting snow;
But the sun can shine in December too,
And this is the time of my gift to you.
   See here, see here,
   My flowers appear!

The swallows have flown beyond the sea,
But friendly Robin, he stays with me;
And little Tom-Tit, so busy and small,
Hops where the jasmine is thick on the wall;
   And we say: "Good cheer!
   We're here! We're here!"

• THE SONG OF •
THE WINTER ACONITE FAIRY

Deep in the earth
I woke, I stirred.
I said: "Was that the Spring I heard?
For something called!"
"No, no," they said;
"Go back to sleep. Go back to bed.

"You're far too soon;
The world's too cold
For you, so small." So I was told.
But how could I
Go back to sleep?
I could not wait; I had to peep!

Up, up, I climbed,
And here am I.
How wide the earth! How great the sky!
O wintry world,
See me, awake!
Spring calls, and comes; 'tis no mistake.

The Winter Aconite Fairy